Brenna Maloney

Photographs by Chuck Kennedy

READY RABBIT GETS READY!

VIKING

An Imprint of Penguin Group (USA)

VIKING
Published by the Penguin Group
Penguin Group (USA) LLC
375 Hudson Street
New York, New York 10014

USA * Canada * UK * Ireland * Australia
New Zealand * India * South Africa * China

penguin.com
A Penguin Random House Company

First published in the United States of America by Viking, an imprint of Penguin Young Readers Group, 2015

LIBRARY OF CONGRESS CATALOGING-IN-PUBLICATION DATA
Maloney, Brenna, author, illustrator.
Ready Rabbit gets ready! / by Brenna Maloney.
pages cm
Summary: Ready Rabbit tries to get ready for school, but he would rather build spaceships
and ride his imaginary motorcycle instead.
ISBN 978-0-670-01549-8 (hardcover)
[1. Imagination—Fiction. 2. Rabbits—Fiction.] I. Title.
PZ7.M29733Re 2015   [E]—dc23   2014015656

Manufactured in China

1 3 5 7 9 10 8 6 4 2

Designed by Kate Renner   Set in Icone Com and Mija

No real rabbits were harmed in the making of this book.
Only one fuzzy sock was slightly mutilated to make Ready Rabbit.

For Liam and Devin,
two rabbits who were born ready

Ready Rabbit isn't feeling very ready.

He is busy dreaming dreams.

But his momma keeps on calling . . .

Ready Rabbit!
It's time to get ready!

so he hops out of bed.

He knows he needs to get ready,
but first he needs to build a spaceship.

Ready Rabbit! You'd better pick up your toys and *get ready*!

scoop

scoop

scoop

Maybe he'd better get dressed before Momma gets mad. What should he wear today?

Handsome green tunic with trusty wooden sword?

Pink prom dress with silky ruffle?

Superhero cape with matching sidekick mask?

Hmmmm . . . all good choices.
But suddenly he remembers
something very important . . .

Rabbits don't wear clothes!

Breakfast!

Breakfast can
be boring.

Saving the life of an incapacitated whale
is *not* boring.

Have you brushed
your teeth yet?

Brushing teeth is important . . .

but so is driving a stagecoach across the Wild West in search of lawbreaking bad guys.

Ready Rabbit! Hurry up!

Oops! Better get busy with those teeth.
Be gentle with the toothpaste. . . .

How *embarrassing*. Ready Rabbit goes back to his room to get more ready . . . sort of.

vroom vroom vroomy

vroom vroom

Ready Rabbit! You'd better not be on your imaginary motorcycle without your imaginary helmet on!

Ready Rabbit is nearly ready.
Time to pack the schoolbag.
Now, what to bring?

"Ready!"

Don't forget
to go potty!

Well . . . almost ready.

Okay. Now he's *really* ready. Ready Rabbit is ready for anything!

BLAST OFF!